Days of the
BLACKBIRD

Days of the
BLACKBIRD

A TALE OF NORTHERN ITALY

TOMIE dePAOLA

G. P. PUTNAM'S SONS
NEW YORK

For Piero Canuto and his family,

both here in New Hampshire and in Sabbia, Italy.

G. P. Putnam's Sons, a division of The Putnam & Grosset Group, 200 Madison Avenue, New York, NY 10016.G. P. Putnam's Sons, Reg. U.S. Pat. & Tm. Off. Published simultaneously in Canada. Printed in Hong Kong. Book Design by Patrick Collins. Text set in Cloister.

Library of Congress Cataloging-in-Publication Data   dePaola, Tomie. Days of the blackbird: a tale of northern Italy / written and illustrated by Tomie dePaola.   p.   cm.   Summary: At the request of a kind duke's loving daughter, La Colomba, a pure white bird, braves the bitter winter of the northern Italian mountains to sing for the gravely ill man. [1. Blackbirds—Fiction. 2. Fathers and daughters—Fiction. 3. Italy—Fiction.] I. Title. PZ7.D439Day 1997   [E]—dc20   96-3371 CIP AC   ISBN 0-399-22929-9   10 9 8 7 6 5 4 3

Many years ago, high in the northern mountains of the country now known as Italy, a duke lived alone with his daughter, Gemma. He was a widower and had brought Gemma up by himself.

The fine house in which they lived stood in the middle of the town, and the doors were open to any and all who had need. For Duca Gennaro was a kind man, who was known to be wise and fair to all.

Every morning, Duca Gennaro
would sit behind his huge table in the
Great Hall and listen to the people
who came with their problems,
arguments, and complaints. From the
time she was a small child, Gemma
had watched her father talk to each
one and seen them leave satisfied and
happy with his advice.

In the afternoons, Gemma would join her father in the courtyard after her studies.

"And what did you do this fine day, *cara*—my sweet one?" Duca Gennaro would ask. Gemma would tell her father all she had done, what she had read, and what new things she had learned from her tutor.

As they sat and talked, the brightly colored birds nestled in the trees would begin to sing. "Ah, listen, my little one," said Duca Gennaro. "*Il concerto*—the concert—has begun." Always one song lifted in the air above the others. It was from a pure white bird, and her song was the sweetest of all. Gemma called her La Colomba.

Duca Gennaro was never happier than when he was in his courtyard with Gemma, listening to the birds serenade them.

But winter came early in these high mountains. As soon as the snow began to fall, and the days grew shorter, the birds left for warmer places in the south. Then Duca Gennaro and Gemma would spend their afternoons together in the Great Hall near a large crackling fire burning brightly in the fireplace.

Snowdrifts would pile higher and higher, and winter seemed to go on

forever. But Duca Gennaro always reassured Gemma that spring would return. "Soon, dear Gemma, the days will get longer, the sun will shine. *La primavera* will come."

"Then the birds will return and you will have *i concerti* again," Gemma told her father.

"Yes," he would say, "I miss my birdsongs."

Just as her father had promised, the snows would melt, the trees would sprout buds, and then one day, the clear song of La Colomba would fly through the windows and into the Great Hall. She was always the first to return. In no time at all, the courtyard was filled with flowers and birds. Duca Gennaro and Gemma would take their places under the trees and listen to the beautiful melodies.

One year, after a hot summer under clear blue skies, Duca Gennaro
fell ill. The doctors were called, but nothing they did seemed to help.
The Duke stayed in his bed, unable to get up.

"Open the window, Gemma, so I can hear *il concerto*," Duca Gennaro
said. The songs of the birds seemed to soothe the Duke. So every
afternoon, Gemma would go to his room and open the window. Together
they listened to the birdsongs, and Duca Gennaro was able to fall asleep.

Gradually the days shortened and the air grew colder. Gemma knew that
winter was on its way. Even now, a dusting of snow covered the courtyard
in the early morning. Gemma saw some of the birds fly off.

"Please, please, *carissimi*—dear ones—stay and sing for my father. He will surely get better if he can hear your music. For it is then that he rests. I will feed you and put baskets in the trees where you can nest and keep warm. *Restate, vi prego*—please stay."

Gemma put out plates of seeds and suet for the birds to eat. She tied baskets to the branches of the trees and filled them with soft wool so the birds would be warm.

Every day the birds sang, and even though the Duke didn't get better, he didn't get worse.

The heavy snowfalls didn't stay away forever. In December, they began. Now more birds left. But La Colomba stayed, and sang longer and sweeter for Gemma and her father.

Soon it would be Natale, Christmas. Every year, Gemma and her father looked forward to Christmas morning. The children from the town would come to the Great Hall for a feast, with *panettone*, hot chocolate, and a small gift for each of them. This year the Duke was too ill to leave his room. "Gemma," he said to his daughter. "You must sit in my chair on Christmas morning and greet the children and give them their gifts." Gemma did as he wished. And La Colomba and the other birds that were still there sang a beautiful song for Natale.

After Christmas, more snow fell, and by the end of Epifania, the Feast of the Three Kings, on January 6, most of the birds had gone. No more yellow birds with their pointy voices, no more blue birds with their voices like flutes. They and the green birds and the deep-rose birds had all flown off to the south.

Finally, in the middle of January, the red birds with their clear trills left too. Only La Colomba was still there.

The Duke's friends knew how much he loved the birdsongs, so they came to the courtyard to play and sing. But it wasn't human songs he wanted to hear, and the music and loud voices only tired him.

Gemma went to the garden wrapped in her warm cloak.

"Please, Colomba, please stay," she begged. "I love my father so much. The doctors told me that he needs the warmth of spring to get well. Your song gives him hope and reminds him that spring will come again soon."

La Colomba stayed.

Now it was near the end of
January, the coldest days of the year.
Bitter winds swirled around the
mountain peaks, and the houses
shuddered with the cold.

Still, every afternoon Gemma would open the window a crack, sit on her father's bed, and hold his frail hand while La Colomba sang her song loudly and clearly.

On January 28, the weather turned
even more frigid. Inside the house,
a fire blazed in the fireplace, and
Gemma moved her father into the
Great Hall. Outside, the basket
of wool couldn't keep La Colomba
warm. Gemma opened the window
and La Colomba flew onto the sill,
where the warm air from the fire
could reach her. She started to sing
her song and did not stop until
darkness fell.

Then she flew to the top of the chimney, where the heat from the fire reached up to the bricks, and she nestled down in the warmth. For the next two days, La Colomba stayed in the chimney. She left only to eat and to sing for Duca Gennaro. He had fallen into a deep, feverish sleep, and Gemma sat by his side day and night.

On the third day, the last day of January, La Colomba left the chimney
and flew to the windowsill to sing. Gemma opened the window wide on the
first notes of the song.

What she saw startled her, for the soot had changed La Colomba into a black bird. "*La merla*," Gemma cried. "A blackbird!" But when the bird's song filled the room, she knew it was La Colomba.

The Duke opened his eyes and
sat up for the first time in three days.
He was weak, but whispered, "My
birdsong."

"*Grazie*, Merla," Gemma said.
"Your song has saved my father.
Now I know he will be better."
La Merla flew back to the chimney.

The next morning, a warm wind
blew down the mountain and Gemma
felt spring on its way. The three
coldest days of the year were over.
But La Colomba remained La Merla.
Her feathers were never white again.

On the first warm day of the new year, Gemma and her father were in the courtyard when a red bird arrived. Then a blue one, a yellow, and a green. La Merla was waiting for them. Soon the courtyard was filled once more with song.

LE·GIORNATE·
·DELLA·MERLA·

GENNAIO
·29·30·
·31·

From that year on, La Colomba
would be known as La Merla, and
all her children would be as well.
To honor her, Duca Gennaro
proclaimed that the last three days
in January would thenceforth be
known as Le Giornate della Merla,
the Days of the Blackbird.

And to this day in the mountains
of northern Italy it is the same.

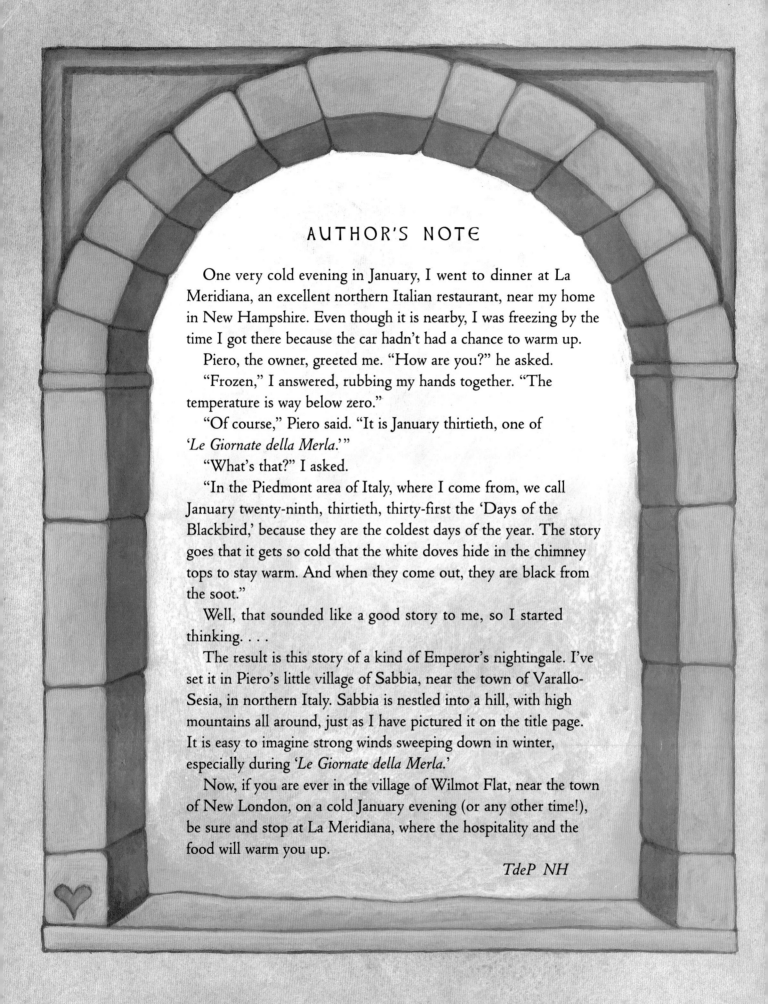

AUTHOR'S NOTE

One very cold evening in January, I went to dinner at La Meridiana, an excellent northern Italian restaurant, near my home in New Hampshire. Even though it is nearby, I was freezing by the time I got there because the car hadn't had a chance to warm up.

Piero, the owner, greeted me. "How are you?" he asked.

"Frozen," I answered, rubbing my hands together. "The temperature is way below zero."

"Of course," Piero said. "It is January thirtieth, one of *'Le Giornate della Merla.'*"

"What's that?" I asked.

"In the Piedmont area of Italy, where I come from, we call January twenty-ninth, thirtieth, thirty-first the 'Days of the Blackbird,' because they are the coldest days of the year. The story goes that it gets so cold that the white doves hide in the chimney tops to stay warm. And when they come out, they are black from the soot."

Well, that sounded like a good story to me, so I started thinking. . . .

The result is this story of a kind of Emperor's nightingale. I've set it in Piero's little village of Sabbia, near the town of Varallo-Sesia, in northern Italy. Sabbia is nestled into a hill, with high mountains all around, just as I have pictured it on the title page. It is easy to imagine strong winds sweeping down in winter, especially during *'Le Giornate della Merla.'*

Now, if you are ever in the village of Wilmot Flat, near the town of New London, on a cold January evening (or any other time!), be sure and stop at La Meridiana, where the hospitality and the food will warm you up.

TdeP NH

jE   De Paola, Tomie.
Depaola
              Days of the
                blackbird.

$15.99   Grades 1-2

DATE			

BAKER & TAYLOR